Growing Seasons

ELSIE LEE SPLEAR

Paintings by KEN STARK

G. P. Putnam's Sons ❖ *New York*

For Carolyn, Clayton, Chris, and Ken

G. P. Putnam's Sons, Reg. U.S. Pat. & Tm. Off. Published simultaneously in Canada.

Printed in Hong Kong by South China Printing Co. (1988) Ltd. Designed by Gunta Alexander. Text set in Nofret.

The paintings for this book were done in casein.

Library of Congress Cataloging-in-Publication Data
Splear, Elsie Lee, 1906-1996. Growing seasons / Elsie Lee Splear; paintings by Ken Stark. p. cm.
SUMMARY: Born into an Illinois farm family in 1906, Elsie Lee Splear describes how she, her parents, and her sisters lived in the early years of the twentieth century and how the changing seasons shaped their existence.
1. Splear, Elsie Lee, 1906-1996. Juvenile literature. 2. Farmers–Illinois Biography Juvenile literature. 3. Farm life–Illinois Juvenile literature. 4. Illinois Biography Juvenile literature. [1. Splear, Elsie Lee, 1906-1996. 2. Farmers. 3. Women Biography. 4. Farm life–Illinois.] I. Stark, Ken, ill. II. Title. CT275.S6256 A3 2000 99-23586 CIP
ISBN 0-399-23460-8   10 9 8 7 6 5 4 3 2 1   First Impression

Preface

Elsie Lee was born into a midwestern farm family in 1906, the third of four daughters.

Elsie's mama and papa were tenant farmers who rented land. They used their combined life savings to buy horses and farm implements, and rented a farm near the small town of Herscher in northeastern Illinois. They had only one daughter, Lillian, but soon she was followed by Mabel, Elsie, and Edna.

At that time, many Americans lived in rural areas, without electricity or indoor plumbing, including Elsie's family.

This book captures Elsie and her family as they lived in the early years of the twentieth century, and how the changing seasons shaped their lives.

Kitchen Stove

The stove was so important to our family that whenever we moved to a new house, the stove was the first thing to be taken off the hayrack and set up in the new kitchen. The next thing we took down was the mailbox, which was set up at the end of the lane.

The kitchen was the center of activity. Mama spent much of her time there, cooking, baking, making butter, washing clothes, or ironing. We did our schoolwork on the kitchen table by the light of the kerosene lamp, and sometimes Mama and Papa read the weekly newspaper while we studied.

The only heat in the house came from the kitchen stove. It was our job to keep the fuel box by the stove full of dry corncobs left over from husking.

We all enjoyed bath night, when Mama filled the tub in front of the stove. Water had to be brought in from the well, using the hand pump outside the kitchen door. All the water for drinking, bathing, and washing clothes and dishes had to be brought in from outside, and we girls learned to carry buckets of water while we were still small. The water was always heated on the stove. We girls took turns getting clean and sometimes one of us read aloud to the others. Mama and Papa took baths after we were done.

Mama in the Garden

We all had our jobs. While Papa and the horses were out in the fields, Mama worked in the garden. She spent part of almost every weekday there, from early spring until fall. She planted and weeded, and sometimes, in hot, dry weather, she had to carry water from the well in watering cans and buckets.

Mama fed our family from the garden and fruit trees. We especially looked forward to picking apples, when the whole family pitched in and collected enough to last until the end of the next summer.

Mama also grew tomatoes, cabbage, carrots, peppers, cucumbers, potatoes, lettuce, all kinds of beans, onions, squash—and sweet corn, which was our favorite. The patches of corn were planted about a week apart, so that they would ripen at different times, and we would have fresh corn to eat throughout the second half of the summer.

Mama canned the fresh vegetables and fruits to be eaten during the winter. She prepared at least four hundred quarts of canned food, which she stored in the cellar. Only flour, sugar, salt, pepper, syrup, and very special items were bought from the store.

When we were tiny, Mama sometimes took us into the garden with her while she worked. One day I was sitting in my high chair, eating a piece of bread when Bowser, one of our family dogs, jumped up to grab the bread and knocked the chair over with me in it. Luckily I wasn't hurt, but poor Bowser felt terrible. Mama had to get me to pet him so he knew I had forgiven him.

Planting Potatoes

The whole family helped Mama in her garden when early spring came and it was time to plant potatoes.

First Papa plowed and tilled the soil while my sisters and I helped Mama cut the seed potatoes into pieces. Each piece had to have a sprouting "eye." When the soil was soft, we went out into the garden with Mama and planted the potatoes in the furrows Papa had made. We used a measuring stick to make sure there was just the right distance between each piece of potato. It took the whole day just to plant the potatoes. Then Papa had to spread the soil over them again.

As the potato sprouts grew, Mama showed us how to hoe gently around each plant and how to pick the insects off the leaves. Finally, in the fall, the time came to lift the potatoes. Papa used the plow to bring them to the surface, and we girls picked up the potatoes one at a time, gently brushing off the loose dirt. We carried them by bushel baskets to a lumber wagon where the potatoes dried. Finally, we stored them in wooden barrels in the cellar. There was always enough to last us through the winter. We loved all the different ways Mama cooked potatoes—fried, boiled, roasted, in soups, in casseroles. I could never decide which was my favorite.

Cow Girls

During summer vacation, my sisters and I looked after the family's cows. We thought of ourselves as cow girls from the Wild West. We milked them twice a day, and herded them in the fresh grass near the farm. We had to stop the cows from eating wild onions because onions would change the taste of the milk Mama used for her butter.

Sometimes when we were herding, my oldest sister, Lillian, brought a storybook to read to us younger girls. I wondered if I would ever know all those words, but Lillian promised that I would when I was a little older.

We also liked to go exploring. One of us kept an eye on the cows while the others went off to see if there were frogs in the creek or some pretty wildflowers in the hedgerow that we could pick to take home to Mama.

Around noon, we walked the cows back to the farm so that they could spend the afternoon in the pasture under the shade trees, chewing their cud.

Wash Day

Monday was wash day. Mama heated water in a copper boiler on the stove. In the boiling water she dissolved slivers of her own soap made from lard, which was animal fat saved at butchering time.

Mama liked to do the wash in a certain order. First she washed the towels and washcloths, then the underwear, nightgowns, and socks. After that came Papa's good shirts and our dresses, and last were the work clothes. Mama changed the water many times. Then everything had to be rinsed and hung outside on the clothesline to dry, when the weather was good. In the winter, the wet clothes were hung in the house to dry. Before she ironed, Mama made starch for the clothes from cooked flour.

Doing the wash took nearly all day, and Mama was often very tired. Sometimes she rested on the couch and watched her wash dancing in the breeze. When we came home from school, we tried to tiptoe into the kitchen so as not to disturb her.

New Car

One evening, Papa made a surprise announcement. "Mama and I think it is time to buy an automobile," he said. "Then Mama will be able to drive into town with the butter and eggs whenever she likes. We'll be able to go on family outings. And it will mean less work for the horses."

Papa had been saving for years. Now he had five hundred dollars, enough to buy a new black Model T Ford. His cousin, who already owned a car, taught him how to drive.

About a month after the car was delivered, he decided to take us all on an outing to a new state park, about sixty-five miles to the northwest. We did our chores in the early-morning darkness and set off on our trip by moonlight. We were wearing our best clothes, and Mama had packed a huge picnic basket full of fried chicken, coleslaw, pickles, buttered bread, peaches, and lemonade.

Just as the sun was coming up, there was a loud noise. The car had a flat tire. I was afraid we couldn't go on with our trip, but Papa was very good with tools. He took off the tire and repaired the tube in just a few minutes. Soon we were on our way again, speeding along at thirty miles an hour with the wind blowing through our hair.

Finally we reached the park. After our picnic, Papa took us on a climb up a high rocky cliff. We could see the river far down below, and Mama waving. We had never been up so high in our lives.

We had to drive home in the dark and do our chores by lantern light, but it was a day I knew I would never forget.

Summer Storms

In the spring and summer, there was always the possibility of severe storms. Everyone kept an eye on the weather. We knew the air could get very still and the birds would become quiet just before a storm. Papa told us, "Watch the dark clouds to see if part of one separates from the rest. That might be the sign of a tornado." If one was on its way, then we always went down to the cellar. Both Mama and Papa had seen tornadoes and other violent wind storms when they were growing up, and they even knew a family whose whole house collapsed in a tornado.

The cellar was the safest place to be during a storm. It had limestone walls and wooden rafters to protect us against fierce winds and heavy rains. We waited out the storm between the wooden shelves of canning jars, crocks of sauerkraut, apple and potato barrels. Papa was the last to come down, and he always brought an ax just in case our house collapsed and we had to chop our way out. Sometimes we had to sleep on the floor, wrapped up in our quilts.

Our poor dog Tippie hated the sound of thunder and the lightning flashes, but he bravely stayed on guard by the cellar door.

Papa's Invention

On the Fourth of July we went into town for the celebration. One year was an extra-special holiday because Papa was going to show off his invention. He had invented a power transmission that would help farmers and their families with everyday chores. Depending on what parts you attached to it, the machine could help pump water, shell corn, fan oats, drill holes, or sharpen tools. Papa had been working on it for years, and Mama had helped with some of the mechanical drawings and with part of the brochure that explained how the machine worked.

We had tacked red, white, and blue bunting around the edges of the hayrack that held the machine, and helped Papa clean the wheels and wipe off the good harness. Then, dressed in his best suit, he stood on the hayrack and drove into town.

When we had finished our chores, some neighbor ladies came in a surrey to take us to join the fun. While Papa showed off his invention, we rode the new merry-go-round, listened to the patriotic speeches and the band playing marches, and watched a hot-air balloon being launched. Just before we left, Mama brought us a chocolate ice cream cone each, which was a rare treat.

Finally, we had to leave to do our chores. Papa didn't get home until after dark with his invention. He told us he'd lost count of the number of men who wanted to talk with him about it. "This," he said, "is one Glorious Fourth I'll never forget."

Milking

Our biggest responsibility was milking the cows. We did this every morning before we went to school, and again in the evening. We had to keep the milk pails and cans clean, as well as the cows themselves.

Each cow had her own name and personality. We wrote their names in chalk on the wooden beam above where they stood to be milked. My favorite was Pansy because she never gave me trouble by trying to kick over the milk pail the way some of the cows did. She even liked the barn cats who wandered around hoping for some spilled milk.

Mama made butter to sell in town. She separated the cream from the milk, and kept it cool in metal cans chained in an underground cistern of cold water. When it was time to make butter, we took turns cranking the wooden churn until it was time for us to go to school. Once the butter was separated from the liquids, Mama put it into a pan of cold water with some salt and kneaded it until it was just the way she wanted it. Then she drained it and stored it in small crocks.

When it was time to sell the butter, Mama drove into town, and often I went with her. I held the butter crocks and the cream cans steady, as well as the eggs from our chickens. We loved going to the store. Sometimes Mama bought soda crackers as a special treat. The store owner was always very pleased to see Mama because some of his best customers asked especially for her butter.

Threshing Day

Threshing day was the busiest day of the year on the farm, and we loved the excitement and all the people who came. Papa belonged to a group of farmers, called a threshing ring, who took turns helping each other harvest grain.

Before the men arrived at our farm, Papa had cut the oats in the field, binding them into shocks for the threshermen to bring up to the farmyard. Sometimes Mama and we girls helped him.

On threshing day, a heavy steam engine pulling the grain separator drove slowly into our farmyard. It ran for the entire day, separating the oats from the straw. Oats were important to the farm because we fed them to the horses, and the farm could not run without horses. The straw was stacked in the hayloft so that it could be used as bedding for both horses and cows.

Papa always had a pile of coal ready to fuel the engine. We loved the smell of burning coal and the feel of the droplets of steam in the air. The steam engine was so loud that when it came near us, we couldn't hear anything else.

At noon, everyone stopped work to eat. We'd been cooking for two days to feed the hungry crew, and there were huge platters of chicken, beef and gravy, potatoes and other vegetables, dishes of homemade pickles and relishes, as well as pitchers of water and lemonade and pots of coffee. For dessert there were apple pies, chocolate cakes, and a large dish of Mama's special rice pudding. Mama made sure my sisters and I kept the plates, cups, and glasses filled. No one ever went away hungry from Mama's threshing day dinner.

When the work was finished and the men had left, we all sat, exhausted, on the back porch steps. The next day Papa would go to help out at another farm, but for that evening we were grateful for a good harvest and for the help and friendship of our neighbors.

Husking

In late fall and early winter, Papa left for the fields about daybreak with the lumber wagon pulled by the horses and Tippie at his side. He tied a kerosene lantern to the wagon, packed several thick jelly sandwiches, and took along a jar of hot coffee, which Mama had wrapped in a winter coat so it would stay warm.

Papa had to harvest the corn by hand. He walked alongside the wagon, cutting each ear of corn off the stalk with a sharp, metal husking hook strapped over his mitten. Then he removed the husk and threw the ear into the wagon, where the bang board stopped it from falling out. Whenever Tippie heard the banging stop, he came running up to see if Papa had a bit of sandwich he might share.

When the weather was bad, the work went slowly. Heavy snow often meant that the ears of corn had to be picked off the ground. Every morning Mama sewed flannel cloths around Papa's wrists, but by evening they were in tatters; his mittens were worn into holes, and his wrists were raw and chapped.

The best ears of corn were saved for next year's crop. Mama stored the seed corn in sacks hanging from the attic rafters.

When we girls came home from school on those cold afternoons, we always heard Papa throwing the ears of corn against the bang board. When we ran to find him, he had a big smile for us. "What did you learn at school today?" he always asked. "Remember, those heads of yours are not just hat racks!"

Butchering

My sisters and I were unhappy when butchering time came around in the late fall. We hated to think of the pigs and chickens being killed, even though we knew all along that they were being raised for food. Mama and Papa promised that the animals would not suffer.

We had to wait until it was good and cold outside so the meat stayed fresh until Mama could cook it. First Papa and a neighbor or two killed one hog at a time, cleaned it, and hung it in the corncrib overnight until the meat was almost frozen. The next night, Mama and Papa cut the meat into smaller pieces and chops.

Our job was to help Mama fry down the pork. We layered the cooked chops in heavy stone crocks and covered them with hot fat. The fat turned to lard as it cooled. This kept out the air and preserved the meat for the winter.

We didn't raise beef cattle, only dairy cows, but sometimes Papa bought or traded for a side of beef from one of the neighbors. Then Mama canned the beef in sealed glass jars so we could use it through the year.

Just before the holiday season, Mama and Papa had enough chickens to sell to a buyer in Chicago. We helped Mama dress them and pack them in new barrels, and then we all went down to the depot to send them to Chicago. I especially liked the hustle and bustle of the railroad station. A few weeks later, when the check arrived in the mail, Mama thanked us for our help.

Christmas

On Christmas Eve, after the chores were finished and we had eaten supper, we each took a bath and then put on our new Christmas dresses. Mama made one for each of us. Then we wrapped up in our winter coats and waited outside with Papa. Mama stayed behind for a minute to open a kitchen window so that Santa Claus could get inside.

We went to Christmas Eve services at Grand Prairie Evangelical Church, several miles away. All of us could see the church windows glowing in the darkness long before we arrived. Inside, a tall, decorated evergreen tree with unlit candles stood in front of the sanctuary.

First there was a Christmas program, and each of the Sunday School classes had parts to recite. We had been practicing our parts for weeks, but I still found it hard to stand up in front of all those people.

After the Christmas prayer, the ushers lit the candles on the tree, using long poles. There were always buckets of water nearby, just in case there was a fire. Everyone, even grown-ups, was given a small, brown paper sack with hard candies, nuts, an apple, and an orange. On the way home, I listened for Santa's sleigh bells. We all hoped Santa had been able to get into the kitchen and that he thought we had been good enough all year to deserve a present.

Inside, Mama lit the kerosene lamp. "Santa came!" she called. There was something for everyone. I got a little tin horse with a cart, Lillian got a baby doll, and Edna, who was the youngest, got a pretty cloth doll with a painted tin head. Mabel had a wind-up train, and Papa put the train tracks together so they ran around the kerosene lamp on the kitchen table. He wound up the train and made it go around the table as we watched. Of course, we did have to get up to do our chores Christmas morning, but I still thought Christmas was wonderful.

Winter Chores

Every morning at four o'clock, Papa was the first out of bed. He started a fire in the stove to warm up the kitchen. Sometimes the kitchen was so cold that the water in the tea kettle had frozen solid. But Papa just put on his boots, heavy coat, wool cap, and gloves and went out to the barn to start his chores.

When he had done about half of them, he came back in for breakfast. Every day he ate pancakes, eggs, and bacon, with coffee. I asked for pancakes too, with butter and syrup. Mama made the best pancakes in the world.

When there was heavy snow, Papa plowed paths around the farmyard. He made one to the barn, one to the corncrib, and another to the privy. Then he had to clear the lane from the road to the house and make paths to the chicken house and the pig shed.

Mama made us wrap up warmly before we went out to do our chores. The snow was so bright, it hurt our eyes, and everything looked like a fairyland as we walked to school. After school, we played in the snow on the way home. Sometimes the drifts were so high that we could walk over the fences.

After the evening chores were done and we had eaten supper, we stayed together in the warm kitchen doing our homework. Sometimes Mama read to us while Papa worked on the plans for a new invention. Then we went upstairs to our beds, warmed by Mama with bricks heated on the stove. We snuggled under our quilts and dreamed of kingdoms of ice and snow.

Another Beginning

When March came around again, it sometimes meant we were going to another farm. Tenant families often moved at this time of year, which fell between the last harvest and spring planting. We moved three times when I was growing up, twice in the same township, but the last move brought us to a farm twenty miles away.

During that move, Lillian was away at high school. Edna rode with Mama in the family car, but Mabel and I had to help Papa keep the cows going forward. Papa led the way with his team of horses, pulling the lumber wagon. He had put a young calf in the back between several bales of straw, and this encouraged the mother cow to follow the wagon, with the rest of the cows following her. A neighbor rode alongside on horseback.

Mabel and I brought up the rear with Tippie. We were worried because we had no idea what to do if the cows decided to turn around and go back to the barn. Luckily they kept going, and finally we arrived, muddy and tired-out, at the new farm. Mama waved from the kitchen door with hot coffee for the grown-ups, sandwiches for us, and a bone for Tippie. Already it was beginning to feel like home.